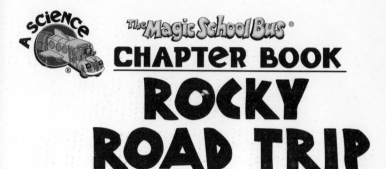

A science

The Magic School Bus®
CHAPTER BOOK
ROCKY
ROAD TRIP

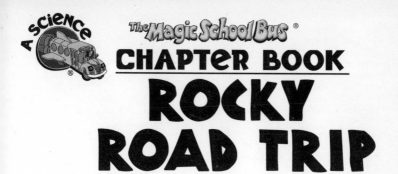

The Magic School Bus®
A science CHAPTER BOOK
ROCKY ROAD TRIP

SCHOLASTIC INC.
New York   Toronto   London   Auckland   Sydney
Mexico City   New Delhi   Hong Kong   Buenos Aires

Written by Judith Bauer Stamper.

Illustrations by Hope Gangloff.

Based on *The Magic School Bus* books
written by Joanna Cole and illustrated by Bruce Degen.

The author and editor would like to thank Dr. John D. Humphrey
of the Colorado School of Mines for his expert
advice in reviewing this manuscript.

ISBN 0-439-56053-5

12 11 10 9 8 7 6 5 4 3   4/0 5/0 6/0 7/0

Designed by Peter Koblish

Printed in the U.S.A.   40

First printing, November 2003

&.INTRODUCTION.•..

Hi, my name is Carlos. I am one of the kids in Ms. Frizzle's class.

You've probably heard of Ms. Frizzle. (Sometimes we just call her the Friz.) She is a terrific teacher, but a little strange.

Ms. Frizzle loves science and will do anything to teach us about it. That's why the Magic School Bus comes in so handy. Believe me, it's not called *magic* for nothing. Once we climb on board, *anything* can happen. And it usually does!

We can tell when a Magic School Bus trip is coming up. How? We just look at what Ms. Frizzle is wearing.

One day, the Friz came into class wearing a dress with rocks all over it.

Since we were studying rocks and minerals, I didn't get suspicious right away. But it didn't take long to find out that a field trip was coming up. We were all in for a *grand* surprise when we found out where we were headed.

Let me tell you what happened when the Magic School Bus took us on a mystery trip to find hidden treasure!

CHAPTER 1.

I staggered into Ms. Frizzle's classroom, carrying my science project in both hands. It was so heavy, I couldn't wait to set it down.

"Carlos," Tim called out. "You look like you're carrying a ton. What's in the box?"

"It's just . . . just my rock collection," I said, trying not to groan. "I found some big ones this weekend."

My muscles were starting to quiver. I had to put the box down soon, or I would have a rock slide on my hands!

THUD! I dropped the collection on top of my desk. A cloud of dust puffed out from the sides of the box.

"I guess if you want to rock, you've got to roll," Dorothy Ann said.

She and Tim laughed, but I just smiled and shrugged. Dorothy Ann — D.A. for short — and Tim know everything about science. They are neck and neck in every science contest we have in class. But this time, I was planning to outsmart them.

I lifted the lid and looked inside my rock collection box.

"Wait until you see my new pieces of sandstone," I said. "I got them from a cliff beside the Saddle River. It's a great spot for rock hounds."

"A great spot for rock heads?" Arnold said, looking confused.

"Not rock heads, Arnold, rock *hounds*," I explained. "You know, people who collect rocks and minerals."

Just then, Ms. Frizzle came into the room, carrying a box labeled SPECIMENS. She headed for the worktable by her desk. Then she turned over the box, and out tumbled a whole bunch of rocks and minerals.

2

Wanna Be a Rock Hound?
by Carlos

   To make a rock collection, you first need to collect some rocks. Look in the school yard, along the banks of a stream, or in a park for rocks of different shapes and colors. Then arrange your specimens in a box or egg carton. Use a field guide to identify the rocks using texture, color, and hardness as clues. Label your collection, then put it on display.

   I ran over to the table to see what was in Ms. Frizzle's rock pile. The rocks were pretty cool, but not as cool as my rock collection. I had been gathering rocks for months. Every year, Ms. Frizzle gives out a Rock Hound of the Year Award to the student with the best science project on rocks and minerals. I was determined to win — and I had a special mystery rock that I was sure could help me do it. The only problem was I didn't know how to identify it.

"Ms. Frizzle," I said, "I brought in my own rock collection. Everything is all organized and labeled."

"That rocks, Carlos," the Friz said with a wink. "Then you can help me sort through this pile."

"I can help, too," Tim quickly added. "I did my project on the three categories of rocks — igneous, sedimentary, and metamorphic."

Rock Solid!

by Tim

What are rocks made of? Other rocks! The amazing forces at work inside and outside planet Earth

---

> continually form new rocks out of old
> ones. Wind, water, and ice can break up
> rocks into tiny pieces. Heat and
> pressure can squeeze, bake, press, or
> melt one kind of rock into another.
> Geologists are scientists who study
> rocks. They sort rocks into three
> categories – igneous, sedimentary, and
> metamorphic – according to the ways
> they were formed.

By now, the rest of the kids had gathered around the worktable. Ms. Frizzle picked up a chunk of rock from the top of the pile. It was black and shiny.

"Meet mystery rock number one," the Friz said. "Everyone check it out. Then try to guess what it is. Think fast," she added, "because this rock is cool."

I moved in closer to inspect the rock. It was sleek and glossy, almost like glass. I could tell from its texture what category it belonged to. I was just about to tell everyone . . . when Tim beat me to it!

"Mystery rock number one is an igneous rock," Tim said. "Right, Ms. Frizzle?"

Igneous Rock

Igneous rock is formed from the hot, liquid rock found deep in the earth's crust. When this molten rock is underground, it is called magma. When it is above ground, it is called lava.

Most igneous rock is very hard. Igneous rock that cools and hardens underground forms slowly and usually has a coarse texture and contains visible crystal grains. Igneous rock that forms above ground cools and hardens faster. It generally has small or even microscopic crystals. Some volcanic rocks cool and harden so quickly that crystals don't have time to form. Those rocks are smooth and glassy.

granite

"Good detective work, Tim," the Friz said.

"It's an igneous rock that formed above ground, right?" I said. "That's why it's so smooth." I wanted to show Ms. Frizzle that I knew just as much about rocks as Tim did.

"Right, Carlos," the Friz said with a smile. "This particular igneous rock is called obsidian. See its sharp edges? Native Americans used obsidian rock to make arrowheads."

"Cool!" Keesha said. She picked up a gray

rock from the table. It broke apart in her hands. "Oops," she said. "What kind of rock was that?"

"It looks like clay!" I said, glancing at Tim to see if he knew the answer, too. "I think it's a sedimentary rock, like sandstone."

Sedimentary Rock

Sedimentary rock is formed by erosion. Erosion is a process where forces such as wind, water, heating, freezing, and gravity break off and move fragments of rock. The rock fragments – along with sand, pebbles, shells, and plant matter – create layers of what is called sediment. Over time, the sediment hardens into sedimentary rock.

Because of the way they were formed, sedimentary rocks often have visible layers or ripplelike markings. They are generally softer than igneous or metamorphic rocks. Some

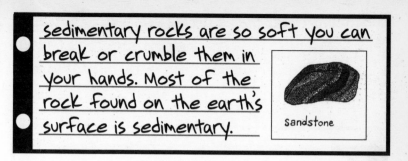

sedimentary rocks are so soft you can break or crumble them in your hands. Most of the rock found on the earth's surface is sedimentary.

sandstone

D.A. looked up from the pad where she had been taking notes. "According to my research, some sandstone is red because it has iron oxides in it."

"Is your hair red because of iron oxides, Ms. Frizzle?" Keesha asked.

"No, Keesha," Ms. Frizzle said with a grin. "My hair is red because my father's hair was red."

"That's called *hair*edity," I added. The class groaned.

Arnold was eyeing a polished white rock on the table. "Is this marble?" he asked, giving the rock a careful poke.

Tim leaned in to look at it. Before I could speak up, he said, "Good call, Arnold. It looks just like the marble sculptures in a museum."

"*Marble*ous!" Ms. Frizzle cried.

"Marble is a metamorphic rock," D.A. told us. "It's formed from a sedimentary rock called limestone."

Metamorphic Rock

Metamorphic rock forms when sedimentary, igneous, or other metamorphic rocks are squeezed and baked by pressure and heat below the earth's surface.

When heat and pressure together form a metamorphic rock, it has layers or bands of crystals that all point in the same direction. When heat alone forms a metamorphic rock, its crystals point in many directions and may not form layers or bands.

marble

D.A. and Tim knew everything about rocks! If this kept going, I would never get the

Rock Hound of the Year Award. I needed to learn more, fast, so I could identify my mystery rock. "Geologists don't just study rocks," I blurted. "They also study minerals."

"What's the difference?" Phoebe asked.

From the Desk of Ms. Frizzle

Rock or Mineral?

What is a mineral? A mineral is a collection of tiny crystals, which are all the same chemical material and all the same shape. There are many different kinds of minerals, each made of a different kind of crystal.

What is a rock? A rock is a collection of one or more different minerals. For example, granite is a rock made from magma that contains the minerals gray quartz, pink feldspar, and black mica.

"Color and texture aren't the only things to look for when you're studying rocks and minerals," Ms. Frizzle said. "There is also a way to test for hardness."

"We can use Mohs' scale," Wanda called out. "I'm doing my project on that."

Mohs' Scale #	Example Mineral	Other
1	talc	
2	gypsum	
2 1/2		fingernail
3	calcite	
3 1/2		penny
4	fluorite	
5	apatite	
5 1/2		glass
6	feldspar	
6 1/2		steel file
7	quartz	
8	topaz	
9	corundum	
10	diamond	

Wanda took out a poster she had made comparing the hardness of the ten different minerals on Mohs' scale. She had also included the hardness of some common things we knew, like a fingernail or a piece of glass.

"The higher the number a mineral has on the scale, the harder it is," Wanda explained. "See? Topaz has a number of eight. That means it can scratch anything with a lower number. But it can be scratched by a mineral with a higher number — like a diamond. Diamonds can scratch almost anything."

"Dazzling!" Ms. Frizzle said. "Here, Wanda, see if you can do a scratch test to identify which of these minerals is harder." The Friz handed Wanda two mystery specimens.

Wanda took the first mineral and scratched it with the second. A white powder fell on the table.

"This first mineral is definitely softer," Wanda said. "Even my fingernail can scratch it. I bet it's talc."

Wanda held the second mineral and

scratched at it with her fingernail. "This one is harder than my fingernail," she said, "so it's not gypsum." She took a penny from her pocket, then dug one edge of it into the mineral. The penny left a scratch.

"This might be calcite, number three on Mohs' scale," Wanda said. "Or, it could be another mineral that has a similar ranking."

"Wanda, that was Mohs-t brilliant!" the Friz said.

I couldn't believe that Wanda knew so much about rocks and minerals! Maybe she would be Rock Hound of the Year. I had to get the Friz's attention back . . . fast.

"Ms. Frizzle," I interrupted. "There's a rock I have that I can't identify. Could I show it to you?"

"There's nothing I love more than a mystery," the Friz said. "Where did you find this rock?"

I ran over to my rock collection and picked up the mystery rock. "I found it in our attic," I said. "My mom said it was my grandfather's. And he always called it the Bright Angel rock."

"Bright Angel?" Ms. Frizzle said. "That's interesting. Bright Angel is the name of a trail in the Grand Canyon."

I handed my Bright Angel rock to the Friz. She took one look at it, and her eyes got as round as saucers.

"What's going on, Ms. Frizzle?" Dorothy Ann said.

"Kids," the Friz said, "I've never found a rock like this before. But I'd like to find more like it! I think it's time for a field trip."

Ms. Frizzle had that special sparkle in her eye. "Come on, Ms. Frizzle," I begged. "What kind of rock do you think it is?"

But the Friz was too busy to answer me. She was already filling her backpack with rock hound tools.

"Follow me," Ms. Frizzle called as she took off out the door, with Liz right behind her. "We're headed for the Grand Canyon. And the Rock Hound *Rock*-et is waiting for us!"

CHAPTER 2

We ran out into the parking lot after Ms. Frizzle. She headed straight for the Magic School Bus.

"But I thought we were taking a rocket," I said.

"Just wait till we drive off . . . I mean, blast off," the Friz replied.

I scrambled into the Magic School Bus and sat right behind the driver's seat. The rest of the class climbed in after me.

Arnold looked even more nervous than usual. "Ms. Frizzle," he said, "don't rockets usually go out into space? I thought we were going to the Grand Canyon."

"Don't worry, Arnold," Ms. Frizzle said.

"This rocket isn't leaving the third rock from the sun."

"The third rock from the sun?" Arnold said nervously. "Where's that?"

"Arnold, we *live* on the third rock from the sun," D.A. said. "That's just another name for planet Earth."

The Friz revved up the Magic School Bus's engine. I noticed that it sounded different. And something strange was happening to our seats. Suddenly, we were leaning back, facing straight up toward the sky.

"Buckle up, kids," the Friz ordered. "Are you ready for countdown?"

"No!" Arnold yelled.

"Yes!" everyone else cheered.

"Okay," Ms. Frizzle said. "Since this is the Rock Hound Rocket, we'll count down with the Mohs' scale of hardness. Who remembers it?"

"I do!" Wanda and I yelled at exactly the same time.

"Let's hear it," the Friz said, punching buttons on the control panel.

Third Rock
by Dorothy Ann

Planet Earth is made out of four layers of rock. The outside layer — the one we stand on — is the crust. Earth's crust is hard and solid. It covers the planet like a shell. Below the crust is a much thicker layer called the mantle. The rock in the mantle is very, very hot and dense. Next comes the outer core, a layer so hot that the rock is melted. At the center of the earth is the inner core. The rock in the inner core is squeezed so hard that it's solid.

Inside the Earth

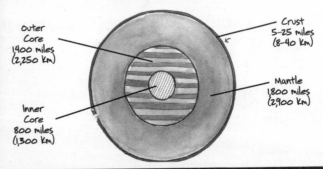

Outer Core
1400 miles
(2,250 km)

Crust
5-25 miles
(8-40 km)

Mantle
1,800 miles
(2,900 km)

Inner Core
800 miles
(1,300 km)

"Ten . . . diamond," Wanda and I started the countdown.

"Nine . . . corundum."

"Eight . . . topaz."

"Seven . . . quartz."

"Six . . . feldspar."

"Five . . . apatite."

"Four . . . fluorite."

"Three . . . calcite."

"Two . . . gypsum."

"One . . . talc!"

"Blastoff!" Ms. Frizzle yelled, pulling down a red lever on the control panel.

Suddenly, the Rock Hound Rocket started to shake. We all grabbed hold of our seats. Then there was a loud roar. Seconds later, the Rock Hound Rocket blasted off, straight into the sky!

I looked out the window. Good-bye, school. Good-bye, Walkerville. Everything kept getting smaller beneath us.

The Friz fiddled with some dials. The Rock Hound Rocket made a 90-degree turn and zoomed straight toward the west.

"Grand Canyon, here we come," I yelled.

"I don't care where we're going," Arnold moaned. "As long as I end up on rock-solid Earth!"

"Ms. Frizzle, why is it called the Grand Canyon?" Phoebe asked. "Is it the grandest canyon of all?"

"I know the answer to that," Keesha said. "I did my science report on the Grand Canyon."

A Great, Big Grand Canyon
by Keesha

Why is it called the Grand Canyon? Because "grand" means big, and the Grand Canyon is the biggest canyon on Earth. How big is it?

Width: At its widest point, the canyon is 18 miles (29 km) wide.

Length: The canyon is 277 miles (446 km) long from end to end.

Depth: The canyon is 1 mile (1.6 km) deep from top to bottom.

I was watching out the window to see if we were coming to the canyon. I wanted to be the first to see it. I couldn't wait to spot a clue that would help me identify my mystery rock.

The Rock Hound Rocket was zooming over a desert. I saw some amazing rock formations down below, but then I saw something that blew my mind away. We were coming up on a big hole in the ground! It was so huge, I couldn't even see the end of it.

"Wow!" I yelled. "That's a whole lot of hole!"

Everybody leaned over to look out the window.

"It looks like a big crack in the earth," Wanda said.

"That's not a crack or a hole," D.A. informed us. "It's the Grand Canyon!"

"Ms. Frizzle," Arnold said in a shaky voice, "we all might crack up if you don't do something about this crazy rocket. It looks like we're headed straight into the canyon!"

"Whoops," Ms. Frizzle said, taking a look

at where the Rock Hound Rocket was headed. "You're right, Arnold. We're headed to rock bottom!"

But the Friz didn't seem worried. She just grinned and punched a button on the control panel.

I looked out the window and saw the Grand Canyon coming closer and closer. What did the Friz have up her sleeve?

We were about to find out. The Rock Hound Rocket started to shake. Just as we were zooming into the canyon, the rocket turned into a helicopter — the Magic School Helicopter. We almost lost our stomachs as the helicopter came to a stop and then hovered in the air.

We had just caught our breath when Ms. Frizzle hit the gas and we took off again. The Magic School Helicopter buzzed through the Grand Canyon like a big insect. First we cruised along the South Rim. Then we buzzed over to the North Rim. Tourists standing along the edge of the canyon waved to us.

"The walls of the canyon look like a rainbow," Ralphie said. "Why do the rocks have all those stripes of color?"

We all crowded around the helicopter's windows to look at the canyon layers. The Friz kept dropping us down deeper and deeper into the canyon. The colors were amazing! We saw layers that were rusty red, creamy white, purple-gray, green, dark brown, and tan. Tim

even spotted some inky black rocks on the canyon floor.

From the Desk of Ms. Frizzle

History Written in Stone

From top to bottom, the Grand Canyon shows its history in twelve layers. Each colorful band of rock was formed during a different period in time. Some of the rock at the bottom of the canyon is over two billion years old! The youngest rock — the top layer — was formed 265 million years ago.

The layers in the canyon contain several different kinds of rocks, including limestone, sandstone, mudstone, shale, mica, quartz, and dolomite. The layers come in many colors, including rusty red, creamy white, purple-gray, green-gray, dark brown, and light tan.

The whole time, I was looking for some bright-colored rock like my Bright Angel rock, but I never saw it. Maybe I'd have to do a close-up inspection.

"Hey, Ms. Frizzle," I said. "Why don't we zoom back up to the top of the canyon? Maybe we should look for Bright Angel up there."

"Bright idea, Carlos," the Friz said. She pulled a lever and the Magic School Helicopter rose up out of the canyon. I watched limestone, sandstone, and shale zoom by us.

At the top of the canyon, the Friz brought the helicopter down for a landing near the edge of the South Rim. We all climbed out of the copter, happy to be on solid ground again. But did we ever get a surprise.

Standing only a few yards away from our helicopter was a national park ranger. She was leading a pack of mules toward the canyon edge. I read the sign that pointed to a trail down into the canyon.

"'Bright Angel Trail,'" I read aloud. "This is it! We've found it!"

CHAPTER 3

"Hi, Ms. Frizzle," the park ranger said. "The mules are all ready for you."

The Friz looked at the amazed expressions on our faces and smiled. "Kids," she said, "meet Marita Chee. She's a park ranger here at the Grand Canyon. I called her before we left school to let her know we wanted to ride down Bright Angel Trail."

We all said hi to Marita. She had big brown eyes and a ponytail of black hair hanging from the back of her ranger hat.

"I'm Carlos," I said. "My aunt's name is Marita. Are you from Mexico, too?"

"My mother's family came from Mexico,"

Marita explained. "But my father's family has lived in Arizona for a long time. The Chees are Native Americans. Later, I'll show you where my ancestors lived."

I wanted to show Marita my Bright Angel rock, but Ms. Frizzle had other plans.

"Okay, kids," the Friz said. "It's time to saddle up!"

"Uh, Ms. Frizzle," Arnold said, "we aren't going to ride into the canyon, are we? No way am I doing that."

"Come on, Arnold," I said, "don't be stubborn as a mule. Climb on!"

Arnold just looked at me and shook his head. No one likes my jokes as much as I do. Well, I was more than willing to take the reins. I put my foot in a stirrup and swung up onto the mule. Suddenly, I had a perfect view of the canyon in front of us. It looked like a bottomless pit! A deep, dark, bottomless pit.

"Uh . . . do these mules know what they're doing?" I asked Marita.

"Not one of them has lost its balance yet," Marita said with a twinkle in her eyes.

"I'm not so sure about this," Arnold said as our mule train started down the canyon.

Part of me agreed with him. The path was steep!

Marita led the way on her mule. I was next in line behind her. Arnold and Ms. Frizzle brought up the rear.

I looked around and felt like I was in rock hound paradise. The Bright Angel Trail zigzagged down the canyon. Sometimes we rode through tunnels in the rock. Sometimes the mules had to pick their way around big

stone formations. Sometimes the trail was so narrow that our mules barely fit on it!

Then Marita brought her mule to a stop. All the other mules stopped, too.

"Look at the canyon wall beside you," she said. "Then run your hand across it. What do you see and feel?"

I took a close look at the grayish-white wall. I knew it was sedimentary rock because I could see how it had formed in layers. The rock had all kinds of things in it.

"I see a shell," D.A. said.

"There's a fish bone," Ralphie added.

"I see a trilobite," I said proudly.

"Does it bite?" Arnold asked nervously.

"A trilobite can't hurt you," I said. "It's been dead for a long time!"

"That's true, Carlos," Ms. Frizzle said. "Hundreds of millions of years ago, when this land was covered in water, insectlike sea creatures called trilobites ruled the earth. There's nothing left of them now but their fossils. And they're not the only creatures that left a rocky record in sedimentary stone!"

From the Desk of Ms. Frizzle

Set in Stone

Rocks have never been alive, but they can hold the remains of plants or animals that once lived. These remains are called fossils. Here are some examples:

mammoth footprint

petrified tree trunk

insect trapped in amber

fish skeleton

trilobite

If you find a fossil in a rock, the rock is probably sedimentary.

"There are a lot more fossils deeper in the canyon," Marita said. Then she kicked her heels against her mule's sides. "Giddyap," she said to her mule. Seconds later, we were all on our way down the canyon again.

The temperature was getting hotter and hotter as we rode deeper and deeper into the canyon. The only sounds we could hear were the calls of birds and the rush of the Colorado River below us.

Marita told us the story of the canyon as we went down. She described how wind and water had carved away the rock over millions and millions of years.

"This ride has seemed like a million years already," Arnold said, wiping the sweat off his brow.

As we neared the river at the bottom, we heard a strange rumble echo through the canyon. Marita stopped the mule train and looked up at the sky. We all looked up, too.

A flash of lightning zigzagged across the sky. Big, dark clouds covered the sun. Thunder roared through the canyon again. The rain started falling so fast that my shirt was soaked in seconds.

"Ms. Frizzle," Marita called out. "We have to get out of here! A flash flood could happen at any minute!"

From Marita's Grand Canyon Guidebook

Flash Flood!

In 1966, 14 inches (36 cm) of rain fell into the Grand Canyon in less than 36 hours. Where did all the water go?

It rushed down the main canyon and into side canyons as a 40-foot-high (12m) wall of mud and water. It tossed huge boulders into the river. It tore out trees like weeds.

In canyon country, heavy rains mean flash floods. Get out before it's too late!

The Friz wasted no time. She whipped a remote control out of her pocket. She aimed it at the top of the Bright Angel Trail where we had begun our ride. We watched as she pushed a red button.

In a minute, we heard a *chop-chop-chop* sound echo in the canyon.

"It's the copter," D.A. said.

We all looked up. The Magic School Helicopter was zooming down the canyon to our rescue. It landed on the trail right behind Ms. Frizzle.

"Get off your mules," Marita yelled. "We've got to get out of here! The mules can run up the trail easier without carrying us."

Arnold slid off his mule, and it took off like crazy up the canyon trail. The rest of our mules followed it.

Just then we heard a terrible roar coming down the canyon from the northeast.

"What is that sound?" I asked Marita.

Marita's face had turned pale. "Flash flood!"

CHAPTER 4

"What do we do?" Ralphie shouted. "There's no way we can fly out of here in this storm!"

I looked at Ms. Frizzle. She had to do something! And she did! She pointed her remote control at the Magic School Helicopter and pressed a red button.

Seconds later, the copter magically turned into a huge yellow river raft.

"Climb into the raft," Marita screamed, trying to make herself heard over the roar of the rushing water. "And put on your life jackets!"

We scrambled into that raft faster than

the mules took off up Bright Angel Trail. And not a second too soon!

The roar of the water coming down the canyon was getting louder and louder. Then, in a flash, it shot around a bend of the canyon—straight at us!

"Hang on!" Ms. Frizzle called. "Here it comes!"

One second we were on the canyon ledge. The next second we were zooming down the canyon on the top of a crest of water.

"Awesome!" I yelled. "This is one grand ride!"

Our big yellow Magic School Raft bounced up and down on the rushing water. The colorful walls of the canyon flashed by us.

"Help!" Arnold yelled. "I got water up my nose!"

"We're lucky we don't all have water up to our ears, Arnold," Marita said. "Just hang on tight, we're coming to some big rapids."

I was sitting at the front of the raft, so I was the first to see them. "White water!" I yelled.

A minute later, we were in the rapids.

Everybody screamed at the same time. It was a wild ride!

Riding the Rapids
by Carlos

The rapids in the Grand Canyon are some of the most dangerous rapids in the world! A rapid is caused by a steep drop in a river's path that causes the water to run faster. When the water surges over rocks at this speed, it creates white water — a sure sign of danger!

Riding the rapids felt like riding a bucking bronco. I just had to make sure I didn't fall off!

The Magic School Raft bobbed up and down through the rapids. I turned around to see how everyone was doing. Arnold was green. The rest of the kids had eyes the size of saucers and were screaming. But Ms. Frizzle had a huge grin on her face.

"Hey, Carlos," she yelled. "How much fun is this?"

"It's a whole raft of fun!" I called back.

Everyone stopped screaming just long enough to groan at my joke.

Seriously, it was a rush. The flash flood carried us on down the canyon. Finally, the river widened and the water became calmer. At the same time, the rain stopped and the sun came out.

"Whew, I'm glad that's over," Marita said. "I checked the weather report before we left, and it didn't say anything about a storm. Usually, you get a little warning!"

"It's a good thing we had our Magic School Raft," Phoebe said. "I just wish we had a Magic School Kitchen. I'm starving."

"This Magic School Raft isn't magic for nothing," Ms. Frizzle said, opening a cooler strapped to the side of the raft. "Peanut butter sandwiches, coming up."

Peanut butter had never tasted so good. While we ate, Marita explained how the Colorado River created the Grand Canyon.

"It all started about 65 million years ago," she said. "Forces deep in the earth lifted up land to form the Colorado Plateau."

"I know what a plateau is," Phoebe said. "I wrote my report on it."

Flat as a Plate
by Phoebe

A plateau is an area of land that is flat on top and higher than the land around it. The word plateau comes from a French word meaning "little plate." But plateaus can be pretty big. The Colorado Plateau is 130,000 square miles (337,000 sq m)!

"For millions of years after the plateau was formed," Marita went on, "the Colorado River flowed across it. And that created a lot of waterpower."

"The river was so powerful," Ms. Frizzle continued, "that it carved a deep canyon through the rock layers that make up the plateau."

"And over time," Marita said, "it formed the Grand Canyon!"

From the Desk of Ms. Frizzle

Waterpower

How can water be so powerful? Gravity pulls water downhill toward sea level. As a river flows over sedimentary rock, bits of dirt, rock, and sand break off. The river carries the debris downstream, and the debris grinds down the rock it travels over. This process is called **erosion.**

That's how the Colorado River carved out the Grand Canyon. But erosion is slow — the process took millions of years!

"But how do you really know that the two sides of the canyon were ever together?" D.A. asked. "Maybe they were always separate."

"Geologists have found proof that they were once together," Marita explained. "And the proof is in the stone. If you look at one side of the canyon and then the other side, the layers match exactly!"

"Cool," I said. "Rock hounds are really smart!"

"You sound like a rock hound yourself, Carlos," Marita said.

I suddenly remembered my Bright Angel rock. I hoped I hadn't lost it in the rapids! I felt around in my pocket and pulled it out.

"This is part of my rock collection," I said proudly. "It belonged to my grandfather. And it's the reason we came out here. My mom always called it the Bright Angel rock."

"So that's why you wanted to go down the Bright Angel Trail," Marita said with a smile. "But there's no rock like that in the Grand Canyon. If there were, all the tourists would be digging for it!"

"What do you mean?" I asked.

"To find your rock, we have to visit a

44

mine . . . and I think I know just the place. My ancestors worked there . . . and it has a special name."

"What's it called?" I asked, beginning to get excited.

"The Bright Angel Mine," Marita said.

❁CHAPTER 5❁

An hour later, we were speeding across the desert in the big yellow Magic School Jeep. The sides of the jeep were open, and we could see everything around us.

"Jeepers," I said. "This is one cool way to get around."

"Carlos," D.A. said. "Your jokes make you sound like a rock head, not a rock hound."

"Hey, look," Tim yelled. "What's that animal?"

We all turned to look at what Tim was pointing to. It was an animal that looked like a cross between a fox and a wolf.

"It's a coyote," D.A. said. "Like Wile E. Coyote in the cartoons."

"And look ahead," Marita said. "There's a roadrunner."

We all laughed at the funny bird speeding along on its long legs.

"How far is it to the Bright Angel Mine?" I asked, eager to find out where my rock came from.

"We won't be there for a few hours," Marita said. "But there are plenty of interesting rocks to see along the way."

"Like those?" Ralphie asked, pointing to some big red rocks sticking up out of the flat desert. "What are they?"

"I know, I know," Keesha said. "I wrote a report on buttes and mesas."

"Very good, Keesha," Ms. Frizzle said. "When we get back to school, maybe you can make some buttes and mesas out of clay."

"I could try, but they won't be as beautiful as Mother Nature's," Keesha said.

She was probably right about that.

Tables and Towers

by Keesha

The desert is dotted with strange, flat-topped mounds and hills. What are they?

A mesa is a flat-topped land-form with steep sides. It looks like a huge table.

A butte is a small mesa that looks like a tower.

Mesas and buttes were once part of a larger, higher piece of rock called a plateau. Over time, wind and water eroded, or wore away, the rock. Mesas and buttes are what's left. In millions of years, they may be gone, too.

Mesa   Buttes

The desert was full of amazing colors and shapes. There were red rock arches and tall rocks sculpted by the wind and water into all kinds of shapes.

"I'm doing my report on geodes," Dorothy Ann said. "Do you think we could find any out here?"

"Ms. Frizzle," Marita said, "when we get beyond that big butte up ahead, turn to the left. There's a place where my uncle used to take me geode hunting as a kid."

A few minutes later, the jeep pulled up to a spot behind the big butte. We all followed Marita as she jumped out of the jeep and headed to a big rock surrounded by what looked like rubble.

"I don't see any geodes," Ralphie said, picking up a brown, round rock. "These are just plain old rocks."

Marita took the rock from his hands and examined it.

"What do you think, D.A.?" she asked.

D.A. pulled a rock hound hammer from her knapsack. She put the rock down on a flat piece of stone and hit it hard with the hammer.

"Gee, a geode!" Ralphie yelled.

D.A. picked up both halves of her geode. Inside were circles of different colored crystals.

"That one is a beauty," Marita said. "See what else you can find, kids."

While we all went geode hunting, D.A. shared her report.

We put our crystal balls into our knapsacks and climbed back into the jeep.

Crystal Balls
by D.A.

How do geodes grow? Here's how these crystal balls are created:

1. Gas bubbles are trapped inside layers of rock. They form holes, or cavities, inside the rock. Water seeps inside the cavities.

---

2. The water evaporates and layers of minerals are left behind. They form on the walls of the cavity.

3. Layer after layer of minerals build up. Each layer may be a different mineral and a different color.

4. When a geode is cracked open, it reveals the beautiful secret inside.

"Where are we going next?" I asked. "To Bright Angel Mine?"

"You'll have to be patient a little while longer, Carlos," Ms. Frizzle said. "There's something else we have to see."

"But you'll enjoy our next stop," Marita said. "It's petrifying!"

"Petrifying?" we all shouted together.

"I don't want to be petrified," Arnold said. "I was scared enough on that mule. And then there was the crazy raft ride. Can't we just go home?"

"Don't worry, Arnold," Ms. Frizzle said. "You won't get petrified. It takes millions of years."

We had no idea what the Friz was talking about. But we soon found out.

We came upon huge fallen trees that stretched out across the sand. The Friz stopped the jeep for us to get out and take a closer look.

"Hey, these aren't real trees," Tim said. "They're hard as rocks."

"They used to be trees," Ms. Frizzle explained. "But now they're stone. They're called petrified wood. It's a kind of fossil."

"Oh," Arnold said with relief. "That's not too scary."

From the Desk of Ms. Frizzle

How Petrifying!

Did petrified trees turn to stone because they were scared to death? No way!

Here's how it happens. Water that is full of a mineral called silica seeps into the tissue of a tree. The water evaporates, leaving behind the mineral. Over time, the tree's tissue is replaced by stone. That's called petrification.

The Petrified Forest in Arizona has a petrified tree that is 220 feet (67 meters) long by 10 feet (3 meters) in diameter.

"*Now* can we go to Bright Angel Mine?" I asked.

Ms. Frizzle and Marita looked at each other. A twinkle came into the Friz's eyes.

"Who wants to see where early Native Americans lived?" she asked. "We can get there fast in the Magic School Jet."

"Let's take off," Tim said. Everybody cheered.

No sooner had we all piled back into the Magic School Jeep than it turned into a plane and taxied across the desert.

Minutes later, we were soaring above the buttes and mesas. They looked like little clay sculptures below us. The plane zoomed along until, suddenly, we saw something amazing below us. There was a whole city built out of rock!

"Is that Mesa Verde?" D.A. asked in an excited voice.

"Yes," Marita said with a proud smile on her face. "Wait until you see the amazing homes the Anasazi people built into the cliffs."

The Friz buzzed the plane close to the cliff dwelling built by the Anasazi. Marita told us the story of the people who had lived there.

From Marita's Notebooks

Cliff Dwellers

The ancient Anasazi people built homes into the high cliffs of the Southwest. At Mesa Verde, the largest of the dwellings, called Cliff House, has over 200 rooms! Archaeologists believe that the cliff dwellings were built between A.D. 450–1300. Now Mesa Verde is a national park that you can explore.

"Now can we go to Bright Angel Mine?" I asked. "I'm itching to find out more about my rock."

"I think it's time to visit my uncle Mica," Marita said. "He can take us there. Ms. Frizzle, we're heading back west."

The Friz lifted the plane higher up into the sky. Soon we were winging our way across the desert.

CHAPTER 6

The Magic School Jet taxied to a stop in the desert. Marita was the first one off the plane. She looked really excited.

"Hurry up, kids," she said. "The trading post closes soon. I don't want to miss my uncle."

Up ahead, I saw an awesome-looking building. The sign above its door read TURQUOISE TRAIL TRADING POST. The place looked right out of a Western movie!

"Where is your rock, Carlos?" Ms. Frizzle asked. "I'll bet Mr. Chee can identify it."

"I've got it right here," I said, patting

my knapsack. "Do you think it might be turquoise?"

"No, Carlos," the Friz said. "I think you might have an even bigger surprise than turquoise."

I was getting more and more curious about my lumpy, yellowish rock. What kind of mine was the Bright Angel Mine?

As we walked up the wooden steps of the trading post, a tall man with gray hair walked out to meet us.

"Marita," he called out. "Who did you bring to visit me?"

Marita introduced us to her uncle, Mica Chee.

"Come on inside," Mr. Chee said.

We followed Mr. Chee into the trading post. The most amazing things were on the walls: Navajo blankets, buffalo heads, jewelry, and arrowheads and flints.

"I'm working on some gemstones," Mr. Chee told us. "I can show you some beauties."

"Is a gemstone a rock?" Phoebe asked.

"I know the answer to that," D.A. broke in.

What a Gem!

by D.A.

Gemstones are a rare kind of mineral. They are beautiful and hard. People value them for their color, and wear them in jewelry.

- A diamond is usually clear with fiery lights.
- A ruby is red.
- A sapphire is blue.
- An emerald is green.
- An opal is milky white with blue, pink, and green highlights.

Gemstones are measured by weight in carats. Long ago, gems were weighed on a balance scale against a pile of carob beans. One carat is roughly the weight of one carob bean. And the word carat comes from the Greek word for carob bean, keration.

"Uncle Mica," Marita said, "will you show the kids your workroom?" As we all followed Mr. Chee into a back room, Marita explained, "Uncle Mica is a famous Native American silversmith. Wait till you see his gems."

Mr. Chee took us into his workroom. Spread out on a table were semiprecious stones of every shape and color.

"That's a garnet," Keesha said. "My birthstone is a garnet."

I spotted an amazing blue stone. It was the color of a deep blue sky.

"Is this turquoise?" I asked Mr. Chee.

"No, it's an even more valuable stone called lapis lazuli," Mr. Chee said. "And do you know how to identify lapis?"

I shook my head. All of a sudden, I realized that I knew a lot about rocks, but not much about minerals!

"Here, I'll show you," Mr. Chee said, picking up the lapis lazuli stone. "One way to identify a mineral or gemstone is called the streak test. Just watch."

From Mica Chee's Notebooks

The Streak Test

You can't always judge a mineral by its color. Some minerals, like tourmaline, can be black, brown, pink, green, or blue. But there is one good way to use color for identification — the streak test. Here's how:

1. Use the rough back of a white ceramic tile.
2. Rub the mineral across the tile.
3. Check out the color of the streak.

The streak of color left on the tile can help you narrow down what the mineral may be. Here is a list of some minerals and the color of their streaks.

Mineral Name	Color of Streak
Tourmaline	white
Green malachite	green
Black hematite	cherry red
Gold	golden yellow
Lapis lazuli	light blue
Pyrite	greenish-black

Mr. Chee scratched the stone against the back of a white tile. Sure enough, it left a light blue streak.

We spent some time using the streak test on other gemstones. Then Mr. Chee showed us his crystal collection. It was out-of-sight! Ralphie had done a report on crystals.

"Excuse me, Mr. Chee," D.A. said. "What are these stones that you set in silver? They are really cool."

"Those are turquoise stones," Mr. Chee explained. "The blue-green color comes from the copper and traces of iron in the stone. Take a look at the different stones. The more iron there is, the greener the stone."

"Why is your trading post called 'The Turquoise Trail'?" Tim asked.

"Because I know where to find deposits of turquoise in the hills around here," Mr. Chee said. "It's a family secret."

"We won't tell!" all of us said at once.

Marita gave us a serious look. "Can we be sure our family secret will be safe?"

Cool Crystals

Mineral crystals are nature's gems. They have flat sides, or faces. You can identify a crystal by the shape of its faces.

Pyrite, also known as fool's gold, is shaped like a cube. Its faces are square.

Pyrite

Beryl, including emerald, has hexagonal, or six-sided, faces.

Beryl

"We'll be as silent as stone, won't we, kids?" Ms. Frizzle said.

"Okay, Uncle Mica," Marita said. "They'll keep your secret. Let's go!"

Mr. Chee smiled and headed to the door, motioning for us to follow.

"Where are we going?" Arnold asked nervously. "And how are we getting there?"

I don't know how the Friz did it, but when we went outside, she was waiting in front of the trading post. And she was sitting on top of the Magic School Stagecoach — drawn by four horses!

"Yippee!" I yelled. "Can I sit up top with you, Ms. Frizzle?"

Before she could say no, I jumped up onto the wooden seat in front of the stagecoach. The rest of the class, along with Mr. Chee and Marita, climbed into the big stagecoach.

"Giddyap!" Ms. Frizzle yelled at the horses.

And we were off! The horses tore across the desert, pulling the bouncing stagecoach behind them. From inside the stagecoach, I could hear Arnold's voice.

"I don't want to see any bandits!" Arnold was yelling. "Get me out of this thing!"

We drove across the desert for an hour. Finally, Mr. Chee stuck his head out of the stagecoach window. "When you see a big red butte standing close to a mesa, steer the horses to the right and rein 'em in."

Ten minutes later, Ms. Frizzle pulled the stagecoach up close to the butte. The horses came to a stop in a big cloud of dust.

"Grab your rock hound tools," Ms. Frizzle said. "You can help collect turquoise for Mr. Chee."

I opened my knapsack and checked my tools.

Soon we were all chipping and chiseling away at the rocks around us. Tim found a big chunk of turquoise that Mr. Chee said was worth hundreds of dollars.

"Mr. Chee, it's amazing to see your family's secret mine," I said. "Can I show you a specimen that's part of my family history?" I pulled my mystery rock from my pocket and

Tools of the Trade
by Carlos

Every real rock hound needs at least two pieces of equipment.

A geologist's hammer has a square head on one side for hammering into rock. The other side of the head has a chisel edge for splitting rocks.

A magnifying lens is used to identify mineral grains. It makes a mineral crystal the size of a pinpoint appear large enough to see.

held it out to him. "It came from my grandfather. We call it the Bright Angel rock."

Mr. Chee took the rock from my hands and turned it over and over. Then he pulled a tile from his pocket. "Why don't you try the streak test?"

I couldn't believe it! I don't know why I didn't think to do the streak test myself. I ran the Bright Angel rock across the back of the white tile, then held it up for everyone to see. D.A. gasped. Mr. Chee smiled. The streak was golden yellow!

My eyes got wide. "Does that mean it's . . ."

"It's time we headed off to the Bright Angel Mine," Mr. Chee said. "Are you ready to search for gold?"

Was I ever!

From the Desk of Ms. Frizzle

Good as Gold

How can you identify real gold? Here's what to look for:
- a hardness on the Mohs' scale of 2.5–3.0 (That means it's pretty soft.)
- a shiny, opaque surface
- a bright gold color
- a golden yellow streak left by streak test

CHAPTER 7

The Magic School Stagecoach tore across the tumbleweed-dotted desert. We followed Mr. Chee's directions down a lonely road that wound through small hills. Ms. Frizzle and I had both put on cowboy hats and bandannas to keep the dust out of our faces.

Suddenly, I saw something that made the hairs on the back of my neck stand up. "Ms. Frizzle, what is that?" I asked, pointing to a group of buildings huddled in a river valley not far away.

"I believe that's a ghost town, Carlos," Ms. Frizzle said. "And Bright Angel Mine must not be far away."

I leaned down to yell into the window of the stagecoach.

"We're heading for a ghost town," I called to everybody.

"Did somebody say ghosts?" Arnold asked.

I didn't hear what Arnold said next because Ms. Frizzle pulled back on the reins, and the horses whinnied as they came to a stop.

"Would you hold the horses, Marita?" Ms. Frizzle asked. "I want to take a picture."

A bunch of us jumped down from the stagecoach and posed for the Friz, but just as she snapped the photo, I heard a spooky wind travel through the ghost town. I wondered if any ghosts would show up on the film when we developed it! We all climbed back on the coach in a hurry. The horses took off running.

Soon we were riding down the main street of the ghost town. We passed an old hotel, a saloon, and lots of abandoned buildings with broken windows and shutters banging in the wind. All the buildings looked ready to fall down.

From the Desk of Ms. Frizzle

Ghost Towns

During the Arizona gold rush of the 1860s, towns sprang up near places where gold was found. The buildings were put together quickly with cheap materials. And when the gold ran out, miners left the towns as fast as they had come. Many ghost towns still stand, with empty streets and spooky buildings. Only a ghost would want to live there!

Mr. Chee stuck his head out of the stagecoach window behind us.

"Ms. Frizzle," he called out, "take the next road to the right that leads down to the river."

"You bet, pardner," Ms. Frizzle said with a tug on her cowboy hat. I was glad to leave that ghost of a town.

The stagecoach bumped down the road to an old wooden bridge over the river. Mr. Chee called out for us to stop before the bridge.

The Friz and I jumped off our seats and tied up the Magic School Horses.

"Follow me over here to that bend in the river," Mr. Chee said to us after everyone had piled out of the stagecoach. "We're going to pan for some gold."

"Why are we looking for gold in a river?" Ralphie asked. "I thought we were going to a gold mine."

"The old gold prospectors found lots of gold in the rivers," Mr. Chee explained. "When the softer rock around gold ore wears away, the gold gets carried by water into riverbeds. It settles down in the stones and sand at the bottom of the water. Here, I have a couple of pans with me. Who wants to try?"

How could we pass up that golden opportunity? D.A., Tim, Phoebe, and Wanda went first. Then Arnold, Ralphie, and Keesha were next. I panned last with Ms. Frizzle.

From Mica Chee's Notebook

Panning for Gold

Here's how to pan for gold:

1. Find a stream near an old gold mine.

2. Use a shallow pan and scoop up the sand and gravel at the bottom of the streambed.

3. Work the pan in a circular motion in the water. The lighter material will go toward the edges.

4. Look at the heavier material that goes to the center and bottom of the pan.

Do you see a shiny yellow grain, flake, or nugget? Do the streak test. If the streak is yellow, you've found real gold.

I scooped up four loads of sand and gravel from the bottom of the riverbed. But I didn't see a sparkle of gold.

"I guess things just aren't going to pan out for you, Carlos," D.A. said with a grin.

I brought up one last scoop of stones and sand. And that's when I saw it! A stone about the size of a marble caught the gleam of the sun.

"I've struck it rich!" I yelled. Everybody came running over to see what I had found.

Are You Fooling Me?
by Carlos

Many prospectors thought they had found gold. But they were wrong! Instead, they had found "fool's gold." That's a nickname for a mineral called pyrite. How do you tell pyrite from real gold? Use the streak test. If it's pyrite, the streak will be black.

Pyrite is good for something, though. For centuries, it was used to make fire. Strike pyrite against flint or iron, and watch the sparks fly!

Mr. Chee picked up the nugget and held it up to the sun. Then he pulled out a tile and did a streak test. "We want to be sure this isn't fool's gold," Mr. Chee said.

It turns out I wasn't a fool. . . . The streak was bright yellow!

"You've got the golden touch, Carlos," Mr. Chee told me. "I think we should head on out to Bright Angel Mine. We'll see what you can find there."

Mr. Chee climbed up on the front of the stagecoach to drive with Ms. Frizzle. I climbed inside to show all the kids my nugget.

Before long, the bouncing of the stagecoach stopped. We all jumped out to see where we were.

"'Bright Angel Mine!'" I read from the old wooden sign hanging over the mine entrance. "This is it!"

"I hope we find buried treasure," Tim said. "I did a report on that!"

"I believe your grandfather must have worked this mine," Mr. Chee said to me. "It's where he would have found that chunk of gold in your pocket. Now let's see if your luck holds out inside the mine!"

Buried Treasure

by Tim

Gold, silver, and platinum are called precious metals. They are rare, beautiful, and expensive. Precious metals can be found in two places:

- in deposits that fill cracks in the earth's crust
- mixed in with sand and gravel at the bottoms of streams

What is the most common use of a precious metal? Silver is used in photographic film. Silver crystals on the film react to light and capture an image. Get the picture?

WARNING!

Mines can be very dangerous. Unless you have a certified mining expert, a world-famous science teacher, *and* a Magic School Bus, steer clear of abandoned mines. *Never* explore one on your own.

At the entrance to the mine, we found an old mine car from the days of the Wild West! It was only big enough for two people — but that wasn't a problem. We were so distracted by the mine that we didn't keep an eye on Ms. Frizzle. When we turned around, we had a big surprise. The Magic School Stagecoach had turned into the Magic School Mine Car.

I ran up to the real mine car and grabbed a spot at the hand pump that made the car go. Ms. Frizzle hopped in beside me.

"Okay," Mr. Chee said as the rest of the kids jumped into the Magic School Mine Car. "Pump that handle, and we'll be inside the mine in no time."

Ms. Frizzle handed out hard hats with lights on the front of them. And we were off! Ms. Frizzle and I led the way, and soon we were zooming through the dark mine. Liz steered the Magic School Mine Car behind us.

"Turn into the tunnel on the left," Mr. Chee called out. "That's where the last gold was found in here."

We made a quick turn to the left and shot through the darkness until we came to the end of the tunnel.

"Okay, everybody out," Ms. Frizzle said. "Here are some hammers to chip out the ore. Start hammering!"

I grabbed a hammer and went over to the wall of stone where the tunnel ended. The light on my hard hat lit up the rock face. I thought I saw what looked like a streak of ore zigzagging through the rock. I hit at it as hard as I could with my hammer.

All around me the other kids were chipping away at the walls of the tunnel.

"Hey, Mr. Chee," I said as my hammer

chipped off a chunk of rock. "I think I may have found —"

Suddenly, my voice was drowned out by a deep rumbling sound. It echoed through the tunnel we had come through. Then the earth felt like it was moving beneath our feet!

"Earthquake!" Mr. Chee yelled out over the rumbling sound. "We've got to get out of here!"

I grabbed the chunk of rock that I had

chipped off and stuck it in my pocket as I ran for the Magic School Mine Car.

"Let's go, class," Ms. Frizzle said. "We haven't a minute to spare!" Ms. Frizzle pushed the red button on her remote control. After that, everything happened faster than a speeding bullet! The mine car turned into a Magic School Bullet Train. We piled in, and the train shot down the tunnel tracks toward the mine entrance. I looked behind us. Rock was crumbling down from the tunnel ceiling and covering the tracks.

"I see light at the end of the tunnel!" D.A. yelled. We shot out of the mine . . . and not a second too soon. There was a giant rumble as rock crashed down and blocked the entrance to Bright Angel Mine.

"Whew, that was a close one!" Ms. Frizzle said.

"Too close for comfort," Marita added. Then she turned to me. "And I'm sorry you didn't have a chance to find gold in Bright Angel Mine just like your grandfather, Carlos."

I felt in my pocket for the rock. Had I

lost it during the earthquake? No — it was still there! With a big smile, I pulled out my rock and held it up in the sunlight.

The sun glinted off the streaks of gold in my rock.

"Carlos," Mr. Chee said to me, "you're as good as gold!"

CHAPTER 8

"That's a magnificent mesa, Keesha," Ms. Frizzle said. "And a beautiful butte."

"Thanks, Ms. Frizzle, but it's not as cool as seeing the real thing," Keesha said.

We were back in the classroom, working on our rocks and minerals projects. Keesha was making a clay panorama of desert rocks. Dorothy Ann was putting the finishing touches on a huge poster about geodes. She had her geode from the desert displayed below it.

I walked over to see what Arnold was doing. He had a sponge cut into the shape of a bone. And he had it sitting in a pan with water and Epsom salts.

"What's that, Arnold?" I asked.

"It's my petrification project," Arnold said. "I was so petrified this whole field trip that I thought it would be nice to see something else petrified for a change."

Arnold explained that the bone-shaped sponge would absorb the minerals in the Epsom salts and then turn as hard as rock. The sponge would turn to stone, just like fossils do.

I headed back to my project, my super-duper rock collection. I had added my gold nugget and my chunk of veined gold from Bright Angel Mine. I was rearranging them one more time when Ms. Frizzle tapped me on the shoulder. When I turned around, Ms. Frizzle was holding something out to me — a T-shirt that read ROCK HOUND OF THE YEAR!

"Yes!" I yelled. "That rocks!"

I pulled the T-shirt over my head. Everyone in the class began to cheer and clap.

"Listen," I said, "I've added something else to my rock hound project."

"We're all ears, Carlos," Ms. Frizzle said.

I turned around and pressed the button on my boom box. The music blasted out, and I jumped up on my desk, holding my piece of gold from Bright Angel Mine.

"This is 'The Rock Hound Rock,'" I said, grinning, "written and sung by the Rock Hound of the Year!"

The class started to clap with me as I sang my song.

The Rock Hound Rock

Check out this rock.
It looks real old.

It might be pyrite.
It might be gold.

Look at its color.
Look at its glow.

Check out its hardness
According to Mohs'.

I did all the tests.
And now I know.

I'm a rocking rock hound
With GOLD to show!

The class cheered. And that was the end of my most awesome field trip ever on the Magic School Bus!

Rock Riddles

1. I'm an igneous rock. I'm black and shiny. I have sharp edges. What am I?
2. I'm a metamorphic rock. I'm used to create beautiful sculptures. What am I?
3. I'm a sedimentary rock. I am a layer of the Grand Canyon from 275 million years ago. What am I?
4. I'm the third rock from the sun. What am I?
5. I look like a plain round rock on the outside. Inside, I have layers of minerals and crystals. What am I?

[Answers: 1. obsidian 2. marble 3. sandstone 4. Earth 5. geode]

Mineral Mysteries

1. I have a hardness of 8 on the Mohs' scale. What am I?
2. I have hexagonal, six-sided, faces. I'm known for my beautiful green color. What am I?

3. I can be black, pink, blue, or green, but I always leave a white streak. What am I?
4. I leave a black streak. I have a cubic shape. What am I?
5. I'm a gemstone used in Native American jewelry. I am green or blue, but if I am blue, I am more valuable. What am I?

[Answers: 1. topaz 2. emerald 3. tourmaline 4. pyrite 5. turquoise]

Join my class on all of our Magic School Bus adventures!